# The Worry Wave

Annette Szproch

NEWMAN SPRINGS PUBLISHING
320 Broad Street
Red Bank, NJ 07701

First originally published by Newman Springs Publishing 2020

ISBN 978-1-64801-614-1 (Paperback)
ISBN 978-1-64801-615-8 (Hardcover)
ISBN 978-1-64801-616-5 (Digital)

Printed in the United States of America

To my sweet nieces Talia and Lexi. May peace be a part of your lives.

"Hey, I'm Sunny the Seagull. It's such a beautiful sunny day out at sea. I love how warm the sun is against my feathers!"

Sunny looks over and sees a dark cloudy section of the sky. He knows he has to see what's going on.

Sunny flies over the big vast sea until he feels the sun hide behind the dark clouds. As he looks down, he sees Billy the Wave looking very upset.

"Hey, Billy, what's going on over here? It's so dark and cloudy!" Sunny flies down to sea level.

"Oh, Sunny, I feel so worried and anxious. My thoughts just keep racing. I feel like I have to always keep up with the other waves. It makes me very sad."

"Billy, I'm sorry you are sad, but why do you feel like you have to keep up?"

"Everyone else has sun shining on them. They all seem so happy. I'm the only wave with darkness above."

Billy the wave is feeling overwhelmed by comparing himself to others! It's time to show Billy he is not alone.

"Billy, it's normal to be sad sometimes. The other waves get sad too. I promise. I have a question. Do you ever watch the other waves crash into shore?"

"Of course! But what does that have to do with how I'm feeling?"

"When the other waves crash at shore, they return back into the ocean. They don't stay at shoreline forever. This is just like your worries. They flow in and out of our minds. They will pass. Worries come and go like waves!"

"But this feels like it will never end. Are you sure, Sunny?"

"I promise! Let's call in our friends to ease your mind."

Sunny shouts into the ocean, "Hey, Lexi the Dolphin, are you out there?"

Lexi swims up. "Hey, Sunny and Billy! What's going on?"

"Billy here is anxious and worried. I'm trying to teach him his worries will pass. Do you have any tips to help our dear friend?"

"Yes! Billy, your worries will come and go like the fish. My favorite tool is taking five deep breaths. Let's all try."

Billy, Sunny, and Lexi all take five deep breaths. The dark clouds above their heads start to slowly break apart.

Billy feels a small ray of sunlight hit his gentle wave body. "I do feel a bit better, but why is the darkness still here?"

Sunny calls in their other friend, Talia, the mermaid.

Talia swims up. "Hey, guys, why is it dark and cloudy here?"

Sunny tells Talia, "Billy is anxious, and we are teaching him tools to help with his worries. I said they won't last forever, and Lexi told him to take five deep breaths. What tools do you use?"

"Yes, Billy, this too will pass! The sun will shine again. What calms me down is telling myself three times,
'I am safe.
It's okay to feel this way.
This will pass.'
Do you want to try, Billy?"
"I guess so."
Talia says, "Come on, everyone, let's all say it together three times."
"I am safe. It's okay to feel this way. This will pass."

As they approach their third round, the dark clouds start to slowly fade away. The sun warms their faces.

Billy starts to smile. "Wow! That really helped calm me down. I thought those dark clouds would never pass. Hey! Look over there! I see dark skies over another wave!"

Sunny says, "I told you, Billy, there are other worried waves out there. We all experience sadness, worry, and anxiety. We just have to remember that it will come and go like a wave at the shoreline."

Billy smiles. "Thank you! Yes, I will remember these tools next time I feel the dark clouds over my head. Thanks for being my friends."

Sunny, Billy, Lexi, and Talia are all enjoying the beautiful sunshine, knowing they always have each other to lean on!

# Mindful Meditation Practice

Next time you feel worried like Billy the Wave, try this meditation:

Close your eyes.

Imagine you are on the beach.

Imagine you are listening to the waves crashing,

watching them come and go.

As you watch the ocean, take five deep breaths very slowly.

Then say to yourself three times,

"I am safe.

It's okay to feel this way.

This will pass."

Repeat until you feel calmer.

# About the Author

Annette Szproch is a yoga and meditation teacher as well as a woman's empowerment coach. She loves all things holistic wellness. She was called to write The Worry Wave while having an anxiety attack one evening and she was reminded of the power of our worries and our emotions. With that she was reminded of the power of our minds and thoughts. She wished that she had tools at a young age to help her navigate the waters of experiencing anxiety, worries, and fears. Annette hopes The Worry Wave can be a navigating tool and provide a mindfulness practice for all children.